© Parragon Book Service Ltd

This edition printed for:
Shooting Star Press, Inc.
230 Fifth Avenue–Suite 1212,
New York, NY 10001

oting Star Press books are available at special
ounts for bulk purchases for sales promotions,
iums, fund-raising, or educational use. Special
ions or book excerpts can also be created to
ecification. For details contact: Special Sales
tor, Shooting Star Press, Inc., 230 Fifth Avenue,
Suite 1212, New York, New York 10001.

ISBN 1 56924 205 4

Printed and bound in Great Britain.

MINI CLASSI

CINDEREL

Sho
disc
prem
edi
sp
Direc

MINI CLASSICS

CINDERELLA

RETOLD BY STEPHANIE LASLETT
ILLUSTRATED BY CAROLINE SHARPE

Once upon a time there was a fine gentleman. He had a young daughter but sadly, his wife died and in time he married again. His new wife was proud and haughty. She had two daughters of her own who were exactly like her in all things. But the man's own daughter was

sweet and good, just like her
dear mother had been.
  Gladly she welcomed her
new relations, hoping they
could all be friendly and
live together happily —
but it was not to be.

No sooner was the wedding over than the stepmother began to show herself in her true colours.

She could not bear her husband's pretty daughter and made her do all the housework. Every day she made her wash the dishes, scrub the tables, sweep the floors and beat the rugs.

Her stepmother and stepsisters were waited on hand and foot and wanted for nothing. Each night the poor girl climbed the stairs to the very top of the old house and there she slept, curled up on a straw bed in the dusty attic. Her sisters had fine rooms, hung with beautiful silk curtains.

There they lay upon soft
beds with perfumed pillows
and satin coverlets.

Each had a large mirror on
their bedroom wall so they
might preen and admire
themselves from head to
foot. But their little stepsister
never had time to look in a
mirror. She was too busy
washing dishes at the sink.

The poor girl had such a
sweet nature that she
carried out her duties with
a smile and never complained.
Her father's new wife now
ruled the house and her
word was law. The little
stepdaughter dared not
moan to her father for she
was afraid of upsetting him.
At the end of the day when

her work was done, the
little girl would sit down
near the warm cinders and
ashes of the kitchen fire
and dream of happier times.

When her stepmother saw
her sitting there she laughed
and called her Cinderwench,
but soon her two stepsisters
had given her a new name:
they called her Cinderella.

But even though little Cinderella was dressed in rags and tatters, she was a hundred times prettier than her sisters in their beautiful gowns. They were so often in a bad temper, and pouted and sulked so regularly, that both their faces had grown quite ugly.

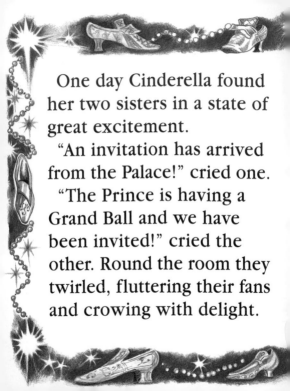

One day Cinderella found her two sisters in a state of great excitement.

"An invitation has arrived from the Palace!" cried one.

"The Prince is having a Grand Ball and we have been invited!" cried the other. Round the room they twirled, fluttering their fans and crowing with delight.

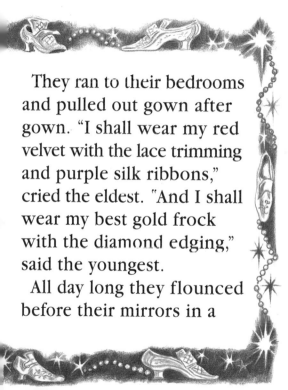

They ran to their bedrooms
and pulled out gown after
gown. "I shall wear my red
velvet with the lace trimming
and purple silk ribbons,"
cried the eldest. "And I shall
wear my best gold frock
with the diamond edging,"
said the youngest.

All day long they flounced
before their mirrors in a

perfect agony of indecision.
"Which shall it be?" they
sighed. "The pretty pink
silk or the yellow brocade?"
Soon the floor was
covered with clothes and
poor Cinderella's heart
sank, for it would certainly
be she who would have to
iron everything smooth
once again.

Bright and early next day the two sisters left the house and went into town. First they called on Mademoiselle de la Poche to discuss their make-up for the Ball. After endless dabbling in pots and gazing in mirrors, they finally left, laden with rouge, powder puffs and beauty patches.

Next they visited the wig-maker and chose new white wigs to wear with fat sausage curls. Smiling contentedly, they returned home, well pleased with their day's shopping.

The day of the Grand Ball finally arrived and the real preparations began. The sisters had not eaten a

thing for two whole days
to be sure that their waists
were as slim as possible.

"Cinderella!" they cried
from their bedchambers.
"Cinderella! Come and
help us dress!" And so poor
Cinderella was called hither
and thither as first one sister,
then the other demanded
help with their clothes.

"Tighter! Tighter!" they cried. And their stepsister pulled with all her strength upon the laces of their bodices but still their waists looked as large as ever.

Over a dozen laces were snapped and two fingernails broken before the sisters finally declared themselves satisfied with the results.

Not once did Cinderella complain. Indeed, she offered to help comb their wigs and the sisters accepted gladly, for her little fingers were more nimble than their own clumsy hands. Carefully they dusted rouge upon their cheeks as Cinderella looked on longingly.

27

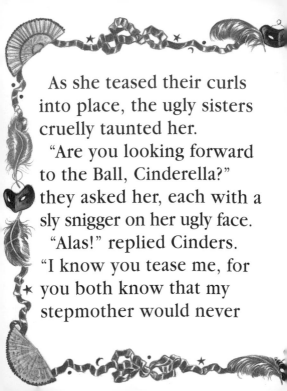

As she teased their curls into place, the ugly sisters cruelly taunted her.

"Are you looking forward to the Ball, Cinderella?" they asked her, each with a sly snigger on her ugly face.

"Alas!" replied Cinders. "I know you tease me, for you both know that my stepmother would never allow me to attend such a grand party."

"Ho, ho!" chortled the sisters. "How everyone would laugh to see such a Cinderella at the Ball. How they would admire your fine dress all tattered and torn! How they would envy your cinder-smudged shoes!" Poor Cinderella!

At last the ugly sisters had spent long enough in front of the mirror and decided they were quite perfect. It was time to leave for the Ball. Down the hall they flounced and Cinderella sadly watched them go.

When they had left the house Cinderella put her head in her hands and wept. Little did she know that her fairy godmother was listening.

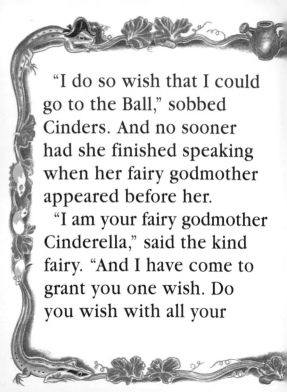

"I do so wish that I could go to the Ball," sobbed Cinders. And no sooner had she finished speaking when her fairy godmother appeared before her.

"I am your fairy godmother Cinderella," said the kind fairy. "And I have come to grant you one wish. Do you wish with all your

heart that you could go to the Ball?"

"Oh, yes please!," cried Cinderella, with a sigh.

"Well," said her godmother, "Just do as I ask and you *shall* go. Quick now! Run into the garden, and bring me a pumpkin." Cinderella ran and found the largest pumpkin. She carried it

back to her godmother, all
the while wondering how
this could possibly help.
Her godmother tapped it
with her magic wand and
the pumpkin was instantly
turned into a fine coach.

"Now fetch me six grey
mice from the mouse-trap,"
ordered the fairy godmother.

One at a time, Cinders let
the mice free and, as they
ran squeaking from the
trap, each was tapped with
the magic wand. Soon six
fine white horses stood
proud and gleaming beside
the golden coach.

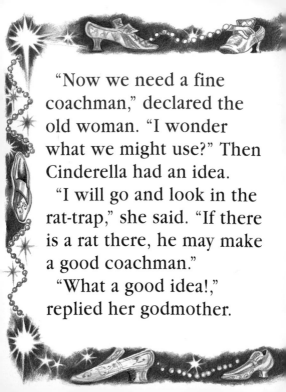

"Now we need a fine coachman," declared the old woman. "I wonder what we might use?" Then Cinderella had an idea.

"I will go and look in the rat-trap," she said. "If there is a rat there, he may make a good coachman."

"What a good idea!," replied her godmother.

Cinderella brought the trap to her, and in it were three huge rats. The fairy inspected them all and finally chose the one with the longest tail.

She touched him with her magic wand and in a flash he was turned into a fat, jolly coachman with smart grey whiskers.

"Now for the footmen," smiled the godmother. "Go again into the garden and you will find six lizards behind the watering-pot. Bring them to me!"

Again the magic wand flashed and the six green lizards were turned into six smart footmen. Each was dressed in a smart green uniform, all embroidered

with gold and silver thread, and splendid green hats now perched upon their heads. They bowed low to Cinders before jumping up behind the coach.

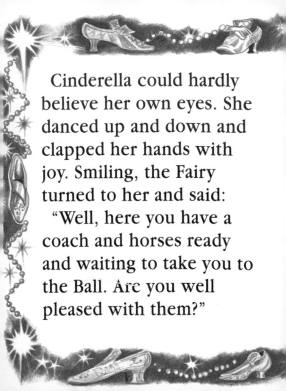

Cinderella could hardly believe her own eyes. She danced up and down and clapped her hands with joy. Smiling, the Fairy turned to her and said:

"Well, here you have a coach and horses ready and waiting to take you to the Ball. Are you well pleased with them?"

"Oh, yes!" cried Cinderella, "but I could not possibly go to a Ball dressed as I am in these horrid rags."

Once again her godmother waved her wand and, in an instant, Cinderella's tatters were turned into a lovely dress of silver and gold and sparkling glass slippers lay on the ground at her feet.

Cindcrella's happiness was complete! But as she climbed into the coach, her fairy godmother warned her that she must be sure to leave

the Ball before midnight, for if she stayed one moment longer, the coach would become a pumpkin again, her fine horses mice, her coachman a rat, her footmen lizards, and her clothes would change back into shabby rags once more.

With a happy smile and a wave, Cinderella promised her godmother that she would not forget. Then the coachman cracked his whip and she was on her way to the Palace.

When she arrived, the King's son was told that an important princess was waiting outside. He ran to

welcome her and gave her
his hand as she stepped
down from the coach.

As the Prince led Cinderella
into the hall, the musicians
lowered their instruments
and everyone stopped
dancing to stare at the
beautiful girl who gracefully
descended the stairs on the
arm of the Prince.

An excited hubbub broke out amongst the guests. "What an exquisite face! Such beautiful hair! Who is she? Who is she?" they cried.

The King and the Queen sat at the end of the hall. Murmuring with open admiration, the dancers parted as the Prince led his lovely new guest across the floor. When they drew near, the old King caught his breath. It was a long time since he had seen such beauty and grace.

As Cinderella passed her ugly sisters, she held her breath. Perhaps they would recognise her! But she had nothing to fear, for the sisters were so dazzled by the splendour of her dress that they saw nothing else.

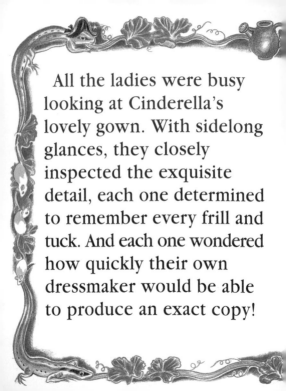

All the ladies were busy looking at Cinderella's lovely gown. With sidelong glances, they closely inspected the exquisite detail, each one determined to remember every frill and tuck. And each one wondered how quickly their own dressmaker would be able to produce an exact copy!

The Prince could not take his eyes off his sweet young companion and all the young ladies looked on enviously as the two of them slowly waltzed around the floor.

When supper was served, the Prince ate not a single morsel, so closely did he watch over Cinderella.

After the meal was over, Cinderella went and sat down by her sisters. With a kind smile she offered them oranges and lemons. The ugly sisters were astonished by her attention and could only gawp, for they did not know this grand lady and they did not think that she knew them.

Then the dancing began again and, whispering sweet words, the Prince asked Cinders to be his partner.

The orchestra played a romantic waltz and the Prince held Cinderella tightly in his arms.

Cinderella was so happy
that she thought her heart
would burst. She closed her
eyes and silently thanked
the fairy godmother who
had made all this possible.

Suddenly her eyes opened
wide. She could hear the
clock striking midnight!
With a gasp, she broke
from the Prince's arms and

ran across the room. All
the guests stared after her
in amazement as she fled
up the stairs and out of the
Palace. Behind her the
chimes of the clock rang
out. One! Two! Three!
Four! Quickly she skipped
down the steps towards
her waiting coach and
horses. Five! Six! Seven!

Eight! Soon she would be
dressed in rags! Faster she
ran and in her haste one
pretty glass slipper fell
from her foot.

Fearful of the time, young Cinderella did not stay to collect her shoe but raced on down the stone steps. Nine! Ten! Eleven! rang out the clock and as she drew near to her coach she heard the final chime.

Twelve! It was midnight! Suddenly the fine gilt coach disappeared and

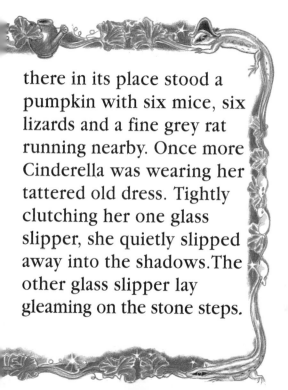

there in its place stood a pumpkin with six mice, six lizards and a fine grey rat running nearby. Once more Cinderella was wearing her tattered old dress. Tightly clutching her one glass slipper, she quietly slipped away into the shadows. The other glass slipper lay gleaming on the stone steps.

Breathlessly, the Prince ran down the steps and turned to his guards.

"Did you see the princess leave?" he gasped.

But they had seen no-one but a poor country girl, all dressed in rags. Later that night the two ugly sisters returned home from the ball. Cinderella sat by the fire and yawned as they bustled into the room.

"What a long time you have been!" she cried as she pretended to rub the

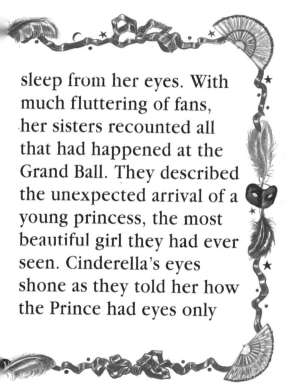

sleep from her eyes. With much fluttering of fans, her sisters recounted all that had happened at the Grand Ball. They described the unexpected arrival of a young princess, the most beautiful girl they had ever seen. Cinderella's eyes shone as they told her how the Prince had eyes only

for her and danced with
no-one else all evening.

"But she seemed to prefer
our company," added her
older sister with a superior
smile and a toss of the head.

"Yes, indeed," agreed the
younger sister. "She sat
beside us and offered us
oranges and lemons from her
own hand." Cinderella hid a

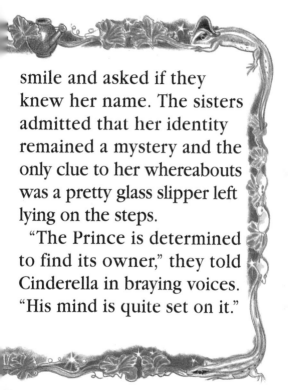

smile and asked if they knew her name. The sisters admitted that her identity remained a mystery and the only clue to her whereabouts was a pretty glass slipper left lying on the steps.

"The Prince is determined to find its owner," they told Cinderella in braying voices. "His mind is quite set on it."

This was indeed very true
and a few days later the
King's son issued a Royal
Proclamation. He would
search all the land until he
found the girl whose foot
exactly fitted the glass
slipper, and then he would
make her his bride.

   And so the slipper was
carried on a velvet cushion
into the Palace and all the
ladies of the Court were
clamouring to try it on.
Grand Duchesses and fine
Ladies fought and squabbled
as they tried to push their
feet into the little slipper.
Soon everyone had tried
their luck but not one had

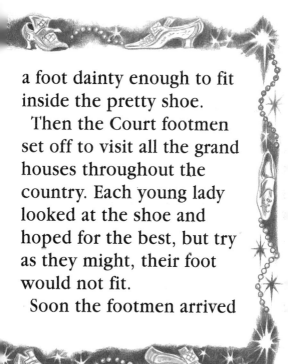

a foot dainty enough to fit inside the pretty shoe.

Then the Court footmen set off to visit all the grand houses throughout the country. Each young lady looked at the shoe and hoped for the best, but try as they might, their foot would not fit.

Soon the footmen arrived

at Cinderella's home. With
loud cries of delight, the
ugly sisters pulled the poor
young men inside. Each was
determined to make the
little slipper fit. Grunting
and groaning, they slowly
squeezed their toes inside
the fragile glass but at last,
with moans of despair,
they had to admit defeat.

Then the footmen spied
Cinderella and insisted she
try on the shoe. Her sisters
watched in disbelief as
Cinderella slipped it onto
her foot. It was a perfect fit!

Their astonishment grew
even greater when little
Cinderella put her hand in
her pocket and pulled forth
the other slipper. The Court
footmen bowed low before
her. This was the Prince's
bride! Then the fairy godmother appeared and in a
flash Cinderella was once
again dressed in her finery.

Now her two sisters could
not fail to recognise the
fine, beautiful lady whom
they had seen at the ball.
They threw themselves at
her feet and begged to be
forgiven for all the ill-
treatment they had made
her suffer. With a merry
laugh, Cinderella drew
them to their feet.

91

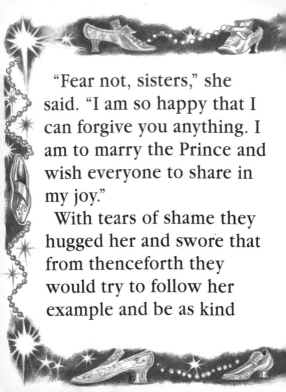

"Fear not, sisters," she said. "I am so happy that I can forgive you anything. I am to marry the Prince and wish everyone to share in my joy."

With tears of shame they hugged her and swore that from thenceforth they would try to follow her example and be as kind

and as loving as she.

Her father and stepmother were soon sharing the good news and soon they were all on their way to the Palace.

The Prince was waiting for her on the steps and soon Cinderella was in his arms. He had found his true Princess at last.

The wedding took place
the very next day as church
bells rang out across the
kingdom. Everyone rejoiced
and made merry but none
was as happy as Cinderella
and her handsome Prince.

CHARLES PERRAULT

Cinderella first appeared in print in 1697 in a
collection of fairy stories written by the French
poet and storyteller, Charles Perrault (1628-1703).
The collection brought together many half-
forgotten traditional folk tales, including
Bluebeard, *Little Red Riding-Hood* and *Puss
in Boots* and together they became known as
Mother Goose's Tales. Written in a simple,
unaffected style, Perrault's stories quickly
became popular in France and later
throughout the world.

There has been considerable dispute over
the years as to the exact author of these tales
and some experts believe that it was actually
Perrault's son, Pierre (1678-1700) who
compiled and recorded the stories for posterity
when he was only 17 or 18 years old.